© KAYE & WARD LTD 1984
© BRITT ALLCROFT LTD 1984

Published by
GRANDREAMS LIMITED,
Jadwin House, 205/211 Kentish Town Road,
London NW5 2JU.

Printed in Holland

ISBN 0 86227 342 0

HELLO!

Hello there!
If you've read any of the stories about Thomas the Tank Engine and his friends, or seen him on television, you'll know who I am. That's right, Sir Topham Hatt — that sounds a bit of a mouthful doesn't it so . . . who is Sir Topham Hatt, did you say? Well, I think you'd better do what Thomas and his friends do, and just call me the Fat Controller. I think they think I don't know their nickname for me, but it seems a shame to spoil their 'secret'.
When I was a young man I

served an apprenticeship at the Great Western Railway's works at Swindon, where one of my friends was a man called William Stanier. Later Stanier moved to the London, Midland & Scottish Railway's works at Crewe, where he designed some splendid engines and became famous as Sir William A. Stanier. Meanwhile, I was helping to build the railway here on Sodor. I was a Director of the Company at first, but when I became Chairman, the engines (not to mention everyone else), began calling me the Fat Controller. To be honest, I quite like it really, but it wouldn't do to let the engines know, would it. It might go to their smokeboxes.

People often wonder if I have a favourite engine. It's a hard question to answer, because if I chose one engine in particular, the others might get jealous. I'm very fond of them all, really. They do their jobs at the right time and in the right places, usually, which is what needs to happen on a properly-run and well-organised Railway.

The other thing people want to know is why we on Sodor stick to steam engines when everyone else has changed to diesel or electric ones. Well, in the first place, not everyone *has* changed, of course, but we still have steam on Sodor because it does the job best, I think. It is true that diesels are useful sometimes, and then we use them, but as long as Thomas and Co are doing an

efficient job I'd be silly to get rid of them, wouldn't I?

And as for electrics, we *have* got an electric railway on Sodor. Did you know that? There haven't been any stories about this line so far, but perhaps one day Mr.

Awdry will write some. For the moment, here are some more tales about Thomas and his friends — I hope you'll enjoy them, along with all the other things about our Railway that you will find in this Annual.

The Fat Controller.

PERCY AND THE CHRISTMAS TREE

It was the day before Christmas Eve. There were to be no trains on Christmas Day and Boxing Day, so Thomas and his friends were looking forward to a nice long rest.

It had been cold and misty all day. Now it was beginning to get dark, and Percy, who was standing at the platform at Ffarquhar, heard a bell ringing. It stopped, and a little later the stationmaster, looking worried, came and spoke to Percy's driver.

"You know the plantation near Hackenbeck?" he said.

The driver nodded.

"The plantation lorry has broken down," the stationmaster went on. "They'd just loaded it with Christmas trees for market at Tidmouth tomorrow, when an axle broke, and it can't possibly be mended in time."

"What do you suggest then?" asked the driver, scratching his head. "That Percy takes some trucks for the stranded trees and then goes on to Tidmouth with them?"

"Bother!" said Percy. "I was looking forward to my nice warm shed."

"Sorry, Percy," said the stationmaster, "but think of the children who might not get a Christmas tree tomorrow if we don't do something about it."

They collected trucks and a guards van from the yard and set off. It was dark now, and because the last train of the day had gone the lights on the Halt at Hackenbeck had been put out. Torches by the lineside showed where the plantation men were waiting. They had unloaded the trees on to a small handbarrow, and pushed them, a dozen or so at a time, to a place where they could be loaded into Percy's trucks.

"Thank goodness you've come," said the Foreman. "Properly saved our bacon you have, and no mistake."

The men loaded the trees as

quickly as they could, but it was very cold, and Percy shivered as he waited. But at last they were ready and Percy puffed off down the valley.

He clattered importantly through the Junction under clear signals, and soon reached the yard at Tidmouth. While his men were unloading the trees, the Foreman came to see Percy. He was carrying a splendid Christmas tree under his arms.

"The men and I thought you might like to have this tree in your shed over Christmas, Percy," he said. "I don't know what we'd have done without you, and I shall write to the Fat Controller to say so. Thank you again, and a very happy Christmas to all of you."

STEP WORD

Illustrated below are 7 characters associated with The Railway Series. If you put the names of 6 of them in the correct order in the grid then the name of the 7th will be found in the heavier ruled boxes. Answers on pages 60-61.

T	H	O	M	A	S		
	E	D	W	A	R	D	
P	E	R	C	Y			
J	A	M	E	S			
G	O	R	D	O	N		
			D	U	C	K	
B	E	R	T	I	E		

OLD GROANER

James was feeling sorry for himself.

"I'm getting old," he grumbled. "I can't get about like I used to. It's all right for you younger ones, but my wheels are getting stiff."

Edward, Gordon and Henry had all been on the Fat Controller's Railway longer than James, but they didn't say so. At last Henry tired of James's complaints.

"Poor old groaner," he said. "It's no use you just sitting there moaning — why don't you tell the Fat Controller that you're past it?"

But James didn't like that idea. Not all old engines, so he had heard, were preserved.

Some, they said, were sold for scrap. James shuddered — he decided not to take a chance on it.

The 'Night Goods' left the big station at midnight. Usually one of the Fat Controller's diesel engines pulled it, but one was away and the other was being mended. James had to take it instead, and he grumbled like anything.

"All this extra shunting," he snorted indignantly.

Two days later an Inspector came to the shed.

"People who live near the yard are complaining," he said. "They say there's a sort of groaning noise which keeps them awake."

"I don't remember hearing anything," said James's driver. "We were there until midnight."

"That's right," agreed the Inspector. "That's when they say it stopped."

"It's probably only James moaning and groaning about his extra shunting," suggested

Henry.

"Shut up!" retorted James. "If you had to shunt at night you'd moan and groan louder than anybody."

That night James's driver and fireman listened carefully.

"It *is* you, James," they said at last. "Your brake-blocks aren't holding your wheels properly, and when they rub against each other they make a groaning sound."

The Fat Controller acted at once.

"I cannot have complaints about my Railway," he ordered. "Tell Donald and Douglas to take turns on the 'Midnight Goods' until the diesels come back. James must have his brakes seen to at once."

James was pleased not to have to pull the night train, but his nickname of 'Old Groaner' stuck for several weeks afterwards. He even began to feel that it might have been better to be doing the shunting!

JAMES THE RED ENGINE

James is a mixed-traffic engine. This means that he can pull trucks just as easily as coaches, but, like most engines he prefers coaches. His wheel-arrangement is 2-6-0 and he is a type built for the Lancashire and Yorkshire Railway, at Horwich, near Manchester. In 1912/13 Mr. Hughes designed a Class 28 Superheated 0-6-0 goods engine. These were powerful, but they tended to be nose-heavy, particularly at speed, so a two-wheeled pony-truck was tried in front of the driving wheels. It was not a complete success, and the idea was abandoned. After the Railway Grouping in 1923, the London, Midland & Scottish Railway, who now owned the L & Y engines, sold one of the 0-6-0s to the Fat Controller, who asked the Works at Crovan's Gate to put back the pony-truck. Since then most things have been corrected, including the wooden brake-blocks with which James was originally fitted, and James has become a useful engine. He has been based at Tidmouth ever since his arrival on Sodor.

COLOUR THIS PICTURE OF JAMES

Draw the picture of Thomas The Tank Engine in the space below, using the squares as a guide. Then colour it in.

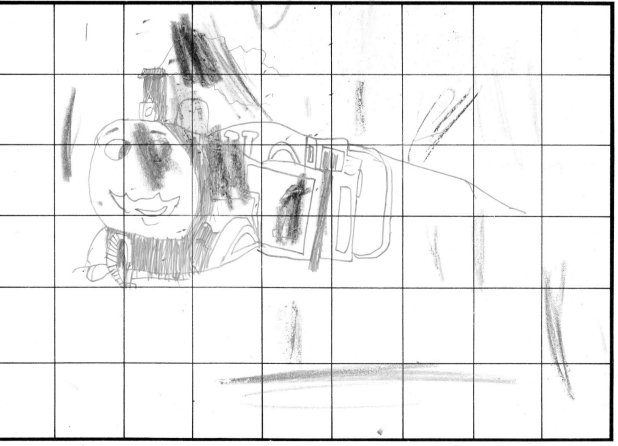

A NUMBER OF NAMES

Each of the engines has a number. By subtracting or adding one to the other, can you find the hidden engine's name? I'll show you what I mean:

Thomas (1) + Percy (6) - James (5) = 2 (Edward)

Here goes then

Edward + Gordon = ...
James + Henry - Gordon = ...
Toby + Thomas - James = ...
Henry + Gordon - Percy = ...

In this puzzle each letter of the alphabet has been given a number, for example
A=1, H=8, L=18 and Z=26
Now find the names hidden in the numbers below:

20, 5, 18, 5, 14, 3, 5   __ __ __ __ __ __ __
16, 5, 18, 3, 25   __ __ __ __ __
7, 15, 18, 4, 15, 14   __ __ __ __ __ __
5, 4, 23, 1, 18, 4   __ __ __ __ __ __
20, 8, 15, 13, 1, 19   __ __ __ __ __ __

JOIN
THE
DOTS

TERENCE TAKES A BATH

Thomas's branch line has a Halt at a place called Hackenbeck. Close to the short wooden platform the line crosses a stream which, in winter, becomes swollen with water from the hills.

One January it rained for almost a week without stopping. The water-level rose in the stream, but no-one realised that a tree-branch had become wedged between the sides of the bridge. Rubbish swept against it forming a dam, and water collecting behind the blockage threatened to wash the bridge away.

A passenger at the station noticed it first, and told Toby's driver.

"Water seems to be higher on

one side than the other," he said.

Toby's driver went to look at once.

"There's a blockage under the bridge," he reported to the stationmaster at Ffarquhar, "but I don't know how we'll shift it. There's no road, so we can't get a crane in."

"Could Terence, with his caterpillar tracks, pull whatever it is free?" asked Toby.

"Probably," agreed the stationmaster. "I'll telephone his owner at once."

Terence was soon on the spot, and after a great deal of cold, wet work, men fixed chains round the branch and shackled the ends to Terence.

"Off you go, Terence," they said. "Gently does it now — heave!"

Terence pulled hard, and slowly the blockage came free. Then suddenly, there was a jerk. Terence's balance shifted, and all at once the bank of the stream collapsed beneath his tracks. It slid into the water, taking Terence with it.

"Ooer!" he groaned. "Help! I didn't want a bath."

His driver tried everything he knew, but Terence's tracks just churned the soil to mud, and he stayed firmly stuck in the stream. The bridge was safe, but Terence wasn't. He was wet, cold and very miserable.

"We need the breakdown train, quickly," said the stationmaster, and he telephoned the Fat Controller.

Thomas was waiting at the Junction, when the stationmaster there said he was to go to Tidmouth. Thomas was surprised, but when the breakdown train was mentioned he knew that it was serious.

"Hurry, hurry, hurry," he puffed as he bustled along the branch line. "I hope none of the engines are hurt."

They stopped at Hackenbeck.

Thomas soon saw the problem, and after manoeuvring the breakdown train into position, waited anxiously while Terence was lifted back to firm ground.

"Thank you, Thomas," said Terence gratefully. "I'll do the same for you one day."

Thomas grinned.

"Remember that snowdrift?" he asked. "That makes us quits, I reckon."

Did you know that 'caterpillar' tracks were first used properly during the First
World War, on tanks, and developed for farm vehicles after the War ended? Terence is
one of these 'caterpillar' tractors, and there is no doubt that his tracks make him a
handy friend to have around. He lives on a farm near Ffarquhar. He and Thomas first
met when Thomas was new to his branch line, just before the winter of snow when
Thomas ran into trouble with a snowdrift. Terence helped him out of that, and a story in
this Annual tells how Thomas repaid the debt. Terence was also on hand to clear the
snow from Mrs. Kyndley's house at the time of Thomas's Christmas Party. Terence
works hard, and though his tracks look old-fashioned these days his owner won't part
with him. "Those tracks have been useful more than once," he says. "You never know
when we might need them again."

PICTURE CROSSWORD

Use the pictures on this page to fill in the squares.

ACROSS

DOWN

A RIDDLE-ME-REE

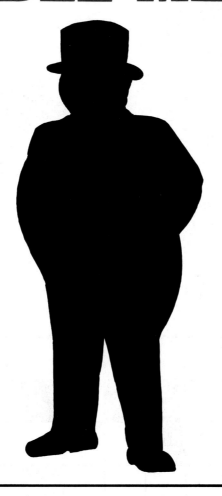

My first is in feather but not in light,
My second's in heather but never in height.
My third is in teacup and also in pot,
My fourth is in crack but never in slot.
My next is in round, but is not seen in ball,
My sixth is in nothing, so can't be in all.
Trucks hold my next, though it isn't in coaches,
My eighth is in porter, in trains and approaches.
My ninth is in nothing but never in nil,
My tenth is in valley and also in hill.
My next shows in lightning but not in the dark,
My twelfth is in cricket but not in the park.
My last is in curves but never in bends,
And my all gives the orders to Thomas and friends.

Who am I?

Answer on pages 60-61

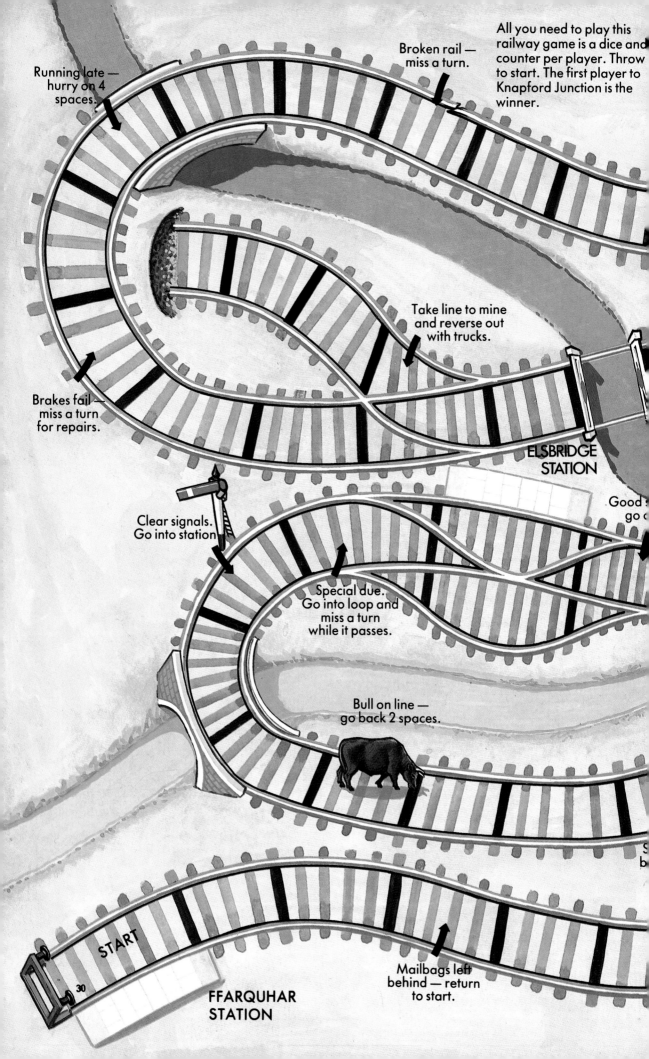

Running late — hurry on 4 spaces.

Broken rail — miss a turn.

All you need to play this railway game is a dice and counter per player. Throw to start. The first player to Knapford Junction is the winner.

Take line to mine and reverse out with trucks.

Brakes fail — miss a turn for repairs.

ELSBRIDGE STATION

Clear signals. Go into station

Good go c

Special due. Go into loop and miss a turn while it passes.

Bull on line — go back 2 spaces.

START

30

FFARQUHAR STATION

Mailbags left behind — return to start.

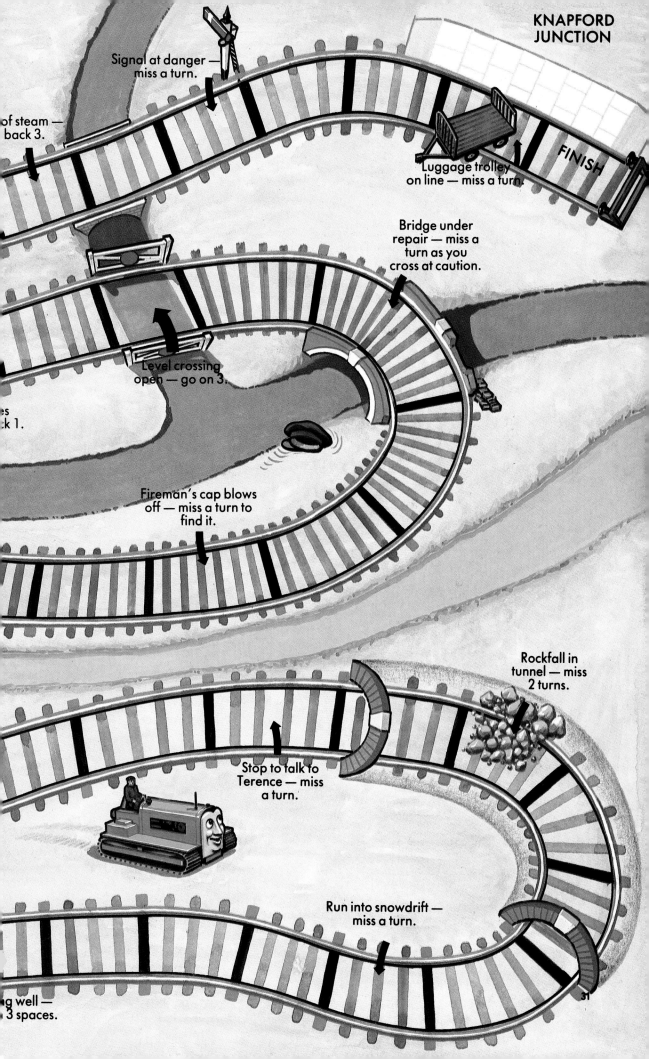

Signal at danger — miss a turn.

of steam — back 3.

Luggage trolley on line — miss a turn.

FINISH

Bridge under repair — miss a turn as you cross at caution.

Level crossing open — go on 3.

es ck 1.

Fireman's cap blows off — miss a turn to find it.

Rockfall in tunnel — miss 2 turns.

Stop to talk to Terence — miss a turn.

Run into snowdrift — miss a turn.

g well — 3 spaces.

31

Percy is a 0-4-0 saddle-tank engine of rather obscure origin. No-one, not even the Fat Controller, really knows where he came from. He was bought second or third hand to help during a locomotive crisis, and is believed to have been originally built by Avonside, at Bristol. However, fitters at Crovan's Gate responsible for his maintenance have now and then found components made by Hunslet, of Leeds . . .! Anyway, however he began life, Percy came to Sodor in 1949, when he was made station pilot at Tidmouth. His early success at keeping Henry and Gordon in their place made him cheeky, but he worked hard, and in 1958 he was transferred to Knapford, to help with the reconstruction of the harbour there. A rake of stone trucks took advantage of him once, pushing him into the sea, but he has remained in charge of freight traffic on Thomas's branch line ever since.

FUNNEL TROUBLE

Oliver didn't feel well.

"I'b all stuffed up id by fuddel," he complained. "I card breath properly."

"Well I gave your smokebox a good clean yesterday," said his fireman. "I'll have a go at your tubes this evening — that might help."

"You sound just like me when I've got a cold," laughed his driver, "but at least you don't keep having to blow your nose like I do."

The fireman cleaned Oliver's tubes, but it made no difference. He brought an Inspector to see Oliver, but the Inspector could find nothing wrong either.

While Oliver was ill Duck had to see to Oliver's ballast wagons. This annoyed him, because it often made him short of time before his first passenger train of the day.

One day, when the trucks were being more troublesome than usual, Duck bumped them. He hadn't meant to, but one of their buffers jammed, and instead of bouncing as it should have done it gave Duck a nasty jolt.

He noticed no ill-effects at the time, but soon after he started his passenger train he began to feel cold and wet above his left-hand wheels.

"That's funny," he remarked to his fireman a few minutes later. "I'm sure I filled right up with water before we started — we can't have used that much already. Look at the gauge."

But the water-level continued to drop, and Duck's driver stopped the train. When they looked, he and the fireman found a steady dribble of water from the corner of one of Duck's tanks.

"You must have loosened a plate when we bumped those trucks," said the driver.

Luckily the middle station was not far ahead, and Bertie's friend Algy took the passengers to Tidmouth. Duck's fireman sent for Oliver.

"Ho, ho, ho," chuckled Oliver. He was still chortling when he was coupled to Duck and they began the journey home.

It was hard work.

"Steady, Oliver," warned his driver. "Don't go putting yourself out of action too."

But just then Oliver felt a sharp pain in his funnel, and something shot out, high into the air. No-one saw it land, but Oliver didn't care. Suddenly he felt well again, and he brought Duck home in fine style.

"You must have had something jammed across your funnel," said the driver. "The extra effort of pulling Duck unjammed it and blew it out. But come on now — your train's due. You'll have no trouble with that now."

JOIN THE DOTS

Bertie came to Sodor quite soon after Thomas was given his branch line. He lived at Ffarquhar, so naturally it wasn't long before his path crossed with Thomas's. That was when Thomas got himself stuck in a snowdrift — while Terence pulled him out, Bertie took the passengers. Soon after that he and Thomas had their race, and that made them firm friends. Bertie was involved in another race too, but that one wasn't planned and Edward didn't even know he was the other competitor. Thomas's fireman was ill, and Bertie promised to take Thomas's passengers to catch Edward's train at the Junction. But Edward didn't know this, and left before Bertie could get there. It was several stations and a telephone call later before an exhausted Bertie managed to catch up. Bertie's owner has another 'bus now, called Algy, to take some of the weight off Bertie's springs.

THE RAILWAY QUIZ

1. What is the name of Toby's coach?

2. How many driving wheels has James got?

3. What colour is Duck?

4. Duck is only a nickname — do you know his proper name?

5. Who once pulled a truck in half?

6. Where is the junction for Edward's branch line?

7. Who once pulled Thomas from a snowdrift?

8. What is the fish train, often pulled by Henry, called?

9. Which engine is no.2?

10. Who fell into Knapsford Harbour?

WHO ARE THEY?

BOYT   ROGNOD   RYNEH

DEWDAR   MOTASH   ENTRENCE

Answers on pages 60-61

COLOUR THIS PICTURE OF THOMAS

GOLDEN OLDIES

Bertie the 'bus and his friends, Thomas and Edward, have been on the Island of Sodor for a long time.

"I never could climb hills well," Bertie would say, remembering his race with Thomas, "but I'll keep going, never fear."

"If you weren't red," laughed his driver, "I'd probably call you a Golden Oldie."

One summer morning Bertie set out on his favourite trip, the Ffarquhar Sunday School outing. He liked being full, but he liked being full of children best.

"It makes a 'bus feel younger," he said.

The party was soon aboard, and Bertie purred happily away. They took the road towards the sea, but stopped in Suddery, the Island of Sodor's capital, to explore the cathedral and the castle. Then, after a picnic lunch, they made for the beach at Brendam, a few miles further on. While Bertie rested in the coach-park his driver joined the children and teachers on the sand.

But during the afternoon one of the teachers began to feel unwell. She said nothing at first, but grew worse and could hide it no longer. By chance one of the other teachers had been a nurse, and diagnosed the trouble at once.

"She should be in hospital as soon as possible," she told the Vicar.

"I'll telephone for an ambulance at once," he said, scrambling to his feet.

"I've a better idea," interrupted Bertie's driver. "There's a direct road to the hospital at Wellsworth from here, so Bertie can be there in no time. Much quicker than an ambulance station and arranged for an extra carriage to be added to the five o'clock train. Edward was surprised to see the children waiting, but was pleased to help.

A train-ride was a bonus for the outing, and the children piled happily into their special coach. Edward puffed off and brought them to the Junction in fine style, where they found Bertie waiting in the yard.

could get here and back, anyway."

"But how do we get the children home," queried the Vicar.

The bus-driver looked at his watch.

"Edward's train leaves at five," he said. "You catch that, and I'll meet you at Wellsworth with Bertie."

So they telephoned the

"Your teacher is quite comfortable," his driver reported. "Bertie did splendidly, and because he got there in such good time the doctor says that the lady should be back at home quite soon."

Bertie grinned happily, and Edward winked at him.

"It's nice to know that some of us oldies are still useful isn't it?" he murmured.

Draw the picture of Henry in the space below, using the squares as a guide. Then colour it in.

Thomas and his friends all visit Crovan's Gate from time to time, because this is where the Fat Controller has built his Locomotive Works, the place where they are repaired. When they go there they often see the engines on Skarloey

Sodor's Little Engines

Railway, a narrow-gauge line that runs to a lake in the mountains. The platform for the narrow-gauge trains is beside the main-line platform, and the little red engines, with their blue and cream carriages (Sir Handel called them cattle-trucks once, but he soon learned his mistake) always have a cheerful word to exchange with the big engines. There are six little engines — Skarloey and Rheneas were built in 1865, Sir Handel in 1878 and Peter Sam in 1921. Duncan is a few years older than Peter Sam, but Duke is older than any of them.

The Thin Controller is in charge of the Skarloey Railway. The line was built to bring down slates from a quarry in the mountains, but holidaymakers are the main traffic now, out for a day in the hills, or sightseeing at the waterfall near the top of the line. Some years ago, when he needed repairs too great for the Fat Controller's Works to do, Skarloey had to go to a factory on the Mainland. There he discovered that both Rheneas and himself had 'Twins', engines exactly like themselves, built at the same place at the same time. What is more, both of them are still working, on a line called the Talyllyn Railway, at Tywyn, in Mid-Wales.

The Talyllyn Railway nearly closed once, but in 1951 a group of enthusiasts took over the running of the line. You can imagine the excitement when, a few years ago, the Manager of the Talyllyn wrote to the Thin Controller saying that Talyllyn was ill and asking if he could possibly borrow an engine. All the Skarloey engines wanted to go, of course: The Thin Controller chose Sir Handel, and he spent two happy summers at Tywyn. He had a wonderful time, but all the same he was glad to come back to his familiar shed at Crovan's Gate when Talyllyn was better. Talyllyn is now back at work, and with Rheneas's 'Twin', Dolgoch, is pulling trains up and down his Welsh valley, just as he has done for 120 years. If you ever go to Tywyn, why not call on him and his friends. They will all be glad to see you.

47

Dilly the Duck lives at one of the stations along the branch line beyond Tidmouth. She became a particular favourite of Donald and her crew, so most people now call her Donald's Duck.

Gordon knew all about Dilly, but thought her beneath his dignity.

"Animals are all very well in their place," he would say loftily, "but they don't help to run a railway."

"The passengers like her," remarked Oliver.

Gordon was not impressed.

"I can't speak for branch lines, of course," he said grandly, "but we main-line engines have a responsibility to keep up. The Fat Controller runs a Railway, not a Zoo."

TOWAWAY

One winter's day Gordon had to visit the Mainland. He shivered as he waited in the Yard there and wished he could get moving and make himself warm again. Just as the signal rose, he thought he felt a sort of scrabbling in his tender, but he hadn't got time to worry about that. He went, as quickly as he could.

Next day was warmer.

Gordon was resting near a platelayers' hut, from which the men had thrown out some scraps after their lunch. A party of sparrows argued noisily over them.

"Go away," ordered Gordon, but the sparrows took no notice.

Gordon was cross.

"Why can't they let an engine rest in peace?" he grumbled.

He tried to blow steam at the birds, but he couldn't without his driver.

Suddenly, something seemed to fly past his smokebox. The sparrows scattered in alarm, and there, on the ground where they had been, crouched a small ginger and white cat.

Gordon was surprised.

"Thank you," he said gratefully. "That's much better."

The cat was friendly. It ate some scraps of meat, and then came and sat on Gordon's bufferbeam. The sparrows twittered noisily at being robbed of their lunch, but they kept a careful distance.

Gordon's driver and fireman laughed when they saw the cat.

"It must have stowed away in your tender on the Mainland yesterday," said the fireman. "I thought I saw something moving, but I was too busy to look properly."

They called the cat Tabitha, and made a great fuss of her. Now she keeps the Shed free from mice, and though she has made friends with the other engines, she always goes to Gordon when she wants a rest.

And in spite of what he said about zoos, Gordon is always glad to see his stowaway.

HELP THE PAINTER!

A

B

C

The painter has been given two cans of blue paint, one of red and one of green, but in the dark he can't tell which engine is which. Can you help him by deciding which of the silhouettes should be red, green or blue? Answers on pages 60-61.

D

WHO AM I ?

You cannot see my boiler
And my dome is hidden as well,
But I've a fine cowcatcher
And a splendid, clanging bell.

Annie and me, we get on fine,
A branch-line work isn't hard.
I hurry up and down the line
With passengers, luggage and Guard.

There's no-one who can pull the Express
Efficiently, like me.
My blue paint is a splendid sight
For everyone to see.

I ran a race with Thomas once,
And came in second place.
But then the Fat Controller said
'It's dangerous to race.'

Answers on pages 60-61

WHO COLLECTS THE TRUCKS?

The Fat Controller has asked one of the engines pictured below to go and collect the trucks. Can you find out which one does? Answer on pages 60-61.

THOMAS   JAMES   PERCY   TOBY   DUCK

A well-tank is an engine which carries its water between its wheels, or sometimes under its cab. A number of 0-6-0 well-tanks, designed by James Holden, were built by the Great Eastern Railway early in this century for working docks and roadside tramways. After the Grouping in 1923 the Great Eastern became part of the London & North Eastern Railway, who re-classified the 'tram' Engines as Class J70. It happened that the Fat Controller needed a tram engine at about the time that Toby's line in England closed. When he arrived in Sodor, Toby had no number, but British Railways withdrew their No 68221 at about the same time he came, in 1951, and we may assume Toby to be that engine: this means that Toby was built in Stratford (London) in 1914. Toby's main responsibility is now the roadside tramway between Ffarquhar and the Anopha Quarry, but he also uses Henrietta to take quarrymen to and from their work.

WORD FIT

Fit the words below into the grid, so that they make a crossword.

3 letters	4 letters	5 letters	6 letters	7 letters
TOP	FLAG	ANNIE	EDWARD	FIREMAN
MUG	LAMP	GUARD	ENGINE	
	NAME			
	TOBY			
	YEAR			
	INCH			
	ACHE			

Answers on pages 60-61

YOU NEVER KNOW

One night in the Shed, Thomas, Percy and Toby were talking about 'buses.

"It was partly the 'buses that closed my old railway," said Toby sadly. "They took away Henrietta's passengers, you see. We never once had an accident, but it made no difference — everyone went by 'bus and nobody travelled in Henrietta."

"A 'bus called Bulgy tried that once with Duck and Oliver," remembered Thomas, "but it didn't work and he's a henhouse now."

"Serves him right," put in Percy. "He got too big for his bonnet."

"I remember when Henrietta once scored over a 'bus," said Toby reminiscently.

"Tell us!" urged Percy.

"It was one summer," Toby began. "The road beside our line was busy. As well as cars going to the seaside, it was market-day in the town and the 'buses were full of people either going shopping or coming home. But there was no-one in poor Henrietta. Driver wanted to leave her behind for the last journey of the day, but I didn't. 'There's no-one in her now, but you never know,' I said.

"Well, we started, and we hadn't gone very far when a 'bus full of people whizzed by much too fast."

"He'll come to a bad end, I shouldn't wonder," said Driver.

"He was right. Before we'd gone another mile we came to a bend. Workmen had been mending gas-pipes, and had dug a deep hole in the road, just around the corner. They had put up warning signs but the 'bus must have been going so fast that it

couldn't stop in time. The signs
were all broken, and the front
wheels of the 'bus were hanging in
mid-air above the hole. The 'bus
couldn't move, and, even if it
could, his front end was so bent
that his driver couldn't have
steered him properly.

"We stopped nearby. The
passengers from the 'bus stopped
telling the driver how careless he
was, and came over to us."

"Can you help?" they asked.

"We want to get home, and this
'bus is no use. Can we come in
Henrietta, please?"

"That's what she's there for,"
replied Driver. "Climb in — Toby
and I will have you home in no
time."

"So Henrietta and I took them
home," finished Toby. "It took a
little longer than no time, I'm
afraid because I can't go very fast,
but wasn't it lucky we took
Henrietta? You never know, do
you?"

Answers Pages

WORD FIT

```
F I R E M A N . E
L . . . . . A . N
A . L . E . M U G
G U A R D . E . I
. M . . W . . . N
T O P . A N N I E
O . . . R . . T .
B . . . D . . C .
Y E A R . A C H E
```

THE RAILWAY QUIZ

1. Henrietta, 2. 6, 3. Green, 4. Montague, 5. Oliver, 6. Wellsworth, 7. Terence, 8. The Flying Kipper, 9. Edward, 10. Percy.

WHO ARE THEY?

Toby, Edward, Gordon, Thomas, Henry, Terence.

WHO COLLECTS THE TRUCKS?

Toby.

PICTURE CROSSWORD

¹T	H	O	²M	A	³S
O			E		H
P		⁴H	A	L	O
⁵H	O	O	T		V
A		R			E
⁶T	U	N	N	E	L

A NUMBER OF NAMES

Edward + Gordon = Percy (2 + 4 = 6), James + Henry − Gordon = Gordon (5 + 3 − 4 = 4), Toby + Thomas − James = Henry (7 + 1 − 5 = 3), Henry + Gordon − Percy = Thomas (3 + 4 − 6 = 1). Terence, Percy, Gordon, Edward, Thomas.

HELP THE PAINTER!

A. James (red), B. Thomas (blue), C. Percy (green), D. Gordon (blue).

STEP WORD

T	H	O	M	A	S
	E	D	W	A	R	D
P	E	R	C	Y	
J	A	M	E	S	
G	O	R	D	O	N
			D	U	C	K
	B	E	R	T	I	E

WHO AM I?

A. Clarabel, B. Toby,
C. Bertie, D. Gordon.

RIDDLE-ME-REE

Fat Controller.